THIS BOOK BELONGS TO:

....

....

....

For Elodie
With love from Mummy and Daddy xxx

SIMON & SCHUSTER BOOKS FOR YOUNG READERS
An imprint of Simon & Schuster Children's Publishing Division
1230 Avenue of the Americas, New York, New York 10020

SIMON & SCHUSTER BOOKS FOR YOUNG READERS
is a trademark of Simon & Schuster, Inc.
For information about special discounts for bulk purchases, please
contact Simon & Schuster Special Sales at 1-866-506-1949
or business@simonandschuster.com.
The Simon & Schuster Speakers Bureau can
bring authors to your live event.
For more information or to book an event, contact the
Simon & Schuster Speakers Bureau at 1-866-248-3049 or
visit our website at www.simonspeakers.com.
Book design by Lucy Ruth Cummins
The text for this book was set in 1820 Modern.
The illustrations for this book were rendered both
digitally and with watercolors.
Manufactured in China
1119 SCP · First Edition
2 4 6 8 10 9 7 5 3 1
Library of Congress Cataloging-in-Publication Data
Names: Scheuer, Benjamin, author. | Williams, Jemima, illustrator.
Title: Hundred feet tall / Benjamin Scheuer ;
illustrated by Jemima Williams.
Description: First edition. | New York :
Simon & Schuster Books for Young Readers, [2020] |
Summary: A rabbit cares for a seed brought home from the countryside
and anticipates being able to climb its branches
one day, so they will both be one hundred feet tall.
Identifiers: LCCN 2018052559 (print) | LCCN 2018057214 (eBook) |
ISBN 9781534432192 (hardcover) | ISBN 9781534432208 (eBook)
Subjects: | CYAC: Seeds—Fiction. | Growth—Fiction. | Rabbits—Fiction.
Classification: LCC PZ8.3.S337 (eBook) | LCC PZ8.3.S337
One 2020 (print) |
DDC [E]—dc23
LC record available at https://lccn.loc.gov/2018052559

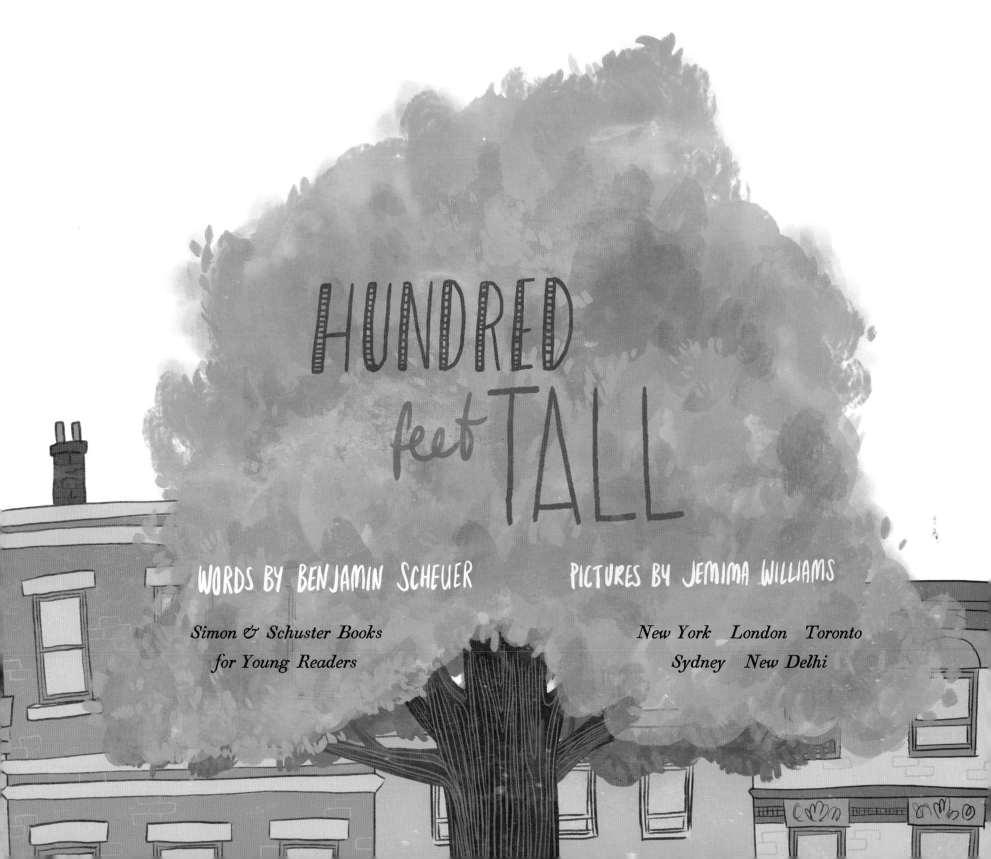

HUNDRED feet TALL

WORDS BY BENJAMIN SCHEUER   PICTURES BY JEMIMA WILLIAMS

Simon & Schuster Books
for Young Readers

New York   London   Toronto
Sydney   New Delhi

Under the tree is a little brown seed
that you find in a dusting of snow.

You pick it up and you bring it inside,
and you promise the seed that you'll help it to grow.

We find a jar and we fill it with earth,
where we plant the seed later that day.

Though we can't see it, it's growing and growing,
and if it could talk it would say . . .

Thanks for the love that you've shown me.
Right now I'm so very small.

But with love and light,
I will keep gaining height.

And then one day

I'll STAND
at a HUNDRED
feet TALL.

Up from the earth grows a little green stalk
with leaves that unfold to the sun.

Under the earth roots are growing and growing.
Something exciting's already begun.

Thanks for the love that you've shown me.
Right now I'm so very small.

But with love and light,
I will keep gaining height.

And then one day

I'll STAND

at a HUNDRED feet

TALL.

If anyone says that
you're too small to matter,
that isn't true.

The love in your heart
that you share with the world

makes a **GIANT** of you.

Now the jar is too small
'cause the tree's grown so big,
from that very small seed
that you found.

We'll take it outside, lift it out of the jar . . .

. . . and we'll plant the tree in the ground.

Thanks for the love that you've shown
to a little brown seed that you found in the fall.

I hope you will visit and and climb in my boughs . . .

. . . and together we'll STAND at a HUNDRED feet TALL.

HUNDRED FEET TALL

Written by
BENJAMIN SCHEUER

VS IA

G | C | G | C | G | D | G | C | G

Un-der the tree is a lit-tle brown seed that you find in a dust-ing of snow. You pick it up and you bring it in-side, and you

7 C | G | D | Em⁷ | C | D | G **VS IB** | G | C | G

pro-mise the seed that you'll help it to grow. You pro-mise you'll help it to grow. We find a jar and we fill it with earth, where we

13 C | G | D | G | C | G | C | G | D

plant the seed la-ter that day Though we can't see it, it's grow-ing and grow-ing, and if it could talk it would say:

CH I

19 C | Em | D | C | B⁷ | Em | C | G

Thanks for the love that you've shown me_____ Right now I'm so ver-y small. But with love and with light I will

24 D | G | C | D | G | C | G | D | G

keep gain-ing height. And then one day I'll stand at a hun-dred feet tall, I'll stand at a hun-dred feet tall

VS II

29 G | C | G | C | G | D

Up from the earth grows a lit-tle green stalk with leaves that un-fold to the sun.

33 G | C | G | C | G | D | Em⁷ | C | D | G

Un-der the earth roots are grow-ing and grow-ing. Some-thing ex-ci-ting's al-rea-dy be-gun. Some-thing's al-rea-dy be-gun.